MW01120021

ETHAN,
A Soccer Player for Jesus

by
Elaine Cunningham

BEACON HILL PRESS
OF KANSAS CITY

Dedication

To young people who share the gospel story
of Jesus Christ in other cultures
through the use of evangelistic soccer balls.

Contents

1. A Great Idea   7

2. The Missing Soccer Balls   12

3. Stuck in the Mud   18

4. The Game   23

5. The Goal   28

Fun Things to Do   32

1
A Great Idea

"Wow! Look at that soccer ball," Ethan whispered to his older sister.

"Shhh," Emily said. "I want to hear what the missionary speaker is saying."

"Me too," said 11-year-old Ethan. He had never seen a soccer ball like the one the missionary was holding.

"We use soccer balls like this one to tell others about Jesus," the missionary said. Instead of a black and white soccer ball, he held up one with five colors: gold, black, red, white, and green. He pointed to the gold color. "Gold stands for God, who lives in heaven where there is no darkness."

Next, the missionary touched the black color. "This dark color stands for sin. The Bible says that all have sinned, and that sin separates us from God."

The missionary turned the ball around until the red color showed. "Red stands for Jesus' blood. Jesus died so our sins could be forgiven, and we would no longer be separated from God.

"When we ask Jesus to forgive our sins, our hearts become clean," said the missionary, pointing to the white color. "White means a clean heart."

Finally, the missionary turned the ball so everyone could see the green color. "Green reminds us to grow in our friendship with God and in love for our neighbors."

As the missionary finished, he tossed the ball to the pastor, who tossed it back to him. "See how easy it is to share the gospel using a soccer ball?" the missionary said.

When the service ended, Ethan grabbed his dad's hand and said, "Let's go talk to the missionary about that soccer ball. Maybe we could take some with us this summer when we go to Costa Rica [KOHS-tah REE-kuh]."

"That's a great idea," Dad said.

Ethan was so excited that he ran ahead of his dad. When the missionary saw Ethan hurrying toward him, he reached out and shook his hand. "Hi, young man. I'm John. What's your name?"

"I'm Ethan. I'm a soccer player."

The missionary smiled and handed the ball to Ethan. "Really? I like soccer too. What position do you like to play?"

"I like playing goalie the best," said Ethan, looking at the soccer ball more closely. "We're going on a mission trip to Costa Rica this summer. I thought it would be fun to take some of these balls with us."

Just then, Ethan's parents and his sister reached the platform and introduced themselves. Missionary John shook hands with them. "Ethan told me you're going on a mission trip."

"That's right. We are planning a trip to Costa Rica with some other families from our church," Mom said.

"Our group is taking equipment to show the JESUS Film," said Dad. "And since Ethan loves soccer, he wondered about taking some soccer balls too. We would use them to share the gospel, play soccer, and then leave them with Christians there to use."

"That would be great," John said. He reached into his pocket for a business card. "Here's the address where you can order the soccer balls. It's www.JFHP.org. They also have basketballs, hacky sacks, and volleyballs with the special colors on them. God is helping us use these tools to bring people to Jesus. May God bless you as you share the gospel in Costa Rica."

"Thank you," said Ethan, as he handed the soccer ball back to Missionary John.

That night, Ethan could hardly sleep. When he finally went to sleep, he dreamed he was playing soccer. The other team had the ball, and they were moving it closer to the goal. Just as the ball flew toward the net, Ethan woke up with the bedsheet wrapped around his neck. He jumped out of bed. "No score!" he yelled. He looked at the clock and grinned. It was almost time for breakfast.

2

The Missing Soccer Balls

Ethan hurried downstairs to the kitchen table. "Mom, don't forget to order the soccer balls."

"I won't," she said, setting a bowl of Cheerios in front of him. "I will order five of them on the Internet today. They should arrive in about a week."

One afternoon when Ethan got home from school, his mother met him at the door. "Guess what," she said. "I think the soccer balls came today. I didn't open the box, though. I thought you'd want to open it, since it was your idea to get the soccer balls."

Ethan carefully cut the tape and opened the box. He lifted one of the flat balls out of the box and discovered an air pump underneath the others. "Cool! They sent a pump so I can pump air into the balls when we get there. I can't wait to play soccer with the kids in Costa Rica!"

"I know," Mother said.

"And I can't wait to tell them about the colors on the ball!" Ethan added, excitedly.

As soon as school ended and summer vacation began, Ethan and his family started packing. Finally, it was time for them to leave.

"I can't stuff one more thing in here," said Ethan, as he zipped his duffle bag. "It's ready to go. Where do you want it, Dad?"

"You can put it in the garage beside the box of soccer balls."

"I wish I could take my shin guards."

Dad laughed. "I don't know where you would put them." He handed Ethan a red ribbon. "Here, tie this ribbon around the box of soccer balls. That will help us find it when we arrive at the airport in Costa Rica."

Ethan carried his bag to the garage and tied the red ribbon around the box. Then he hurried back inside. "Dad, do you have my passport?"

"Mom has our passports. We wouldn't get very far without them. They permit us to travel in other countries."

After loading their luggage and the box of soccer balls into the car, the family headed to the airport.

When everyone in their group arrived, they prayed together. Then they checked their bags and boxes of equipment at the ticket counter and went through security. Ethan took off his sneakers and jacket and put them in a small tub. He watched them go through the X-ray machine. Then he walked through the metal detector.

"Don't forget to collect your shoes and jacket," said the security officer.

The group soon boarded the airplane and prepared for take-off. During the long flight, Ethan and Emily played their handheld video games and talked about the soccer balls.

When the plane landed at the Costa Rica airport, everyone gathered in the baggage claim area. Ethan watched the suitcases, bags, and boxes going around and around. He did not see the box with the red ribbon.

Ethan helped his dad grab their four duffle bags. Soon, all of the luggage and boxes had been picked up—except the box with the red ribbon. The soccer balls were missing!

"Dad, let's ask God to help us find the soccer balls."

"Good idea, Son. Why don't you lead us in prayer."

Everyone in the group gathered around Ethan as he prayed. "Dear God, thank You for helping us get here safely. Please help our soccer balls get here too. Amen."

"Ethan, come with me. We'll report the missing box," Dad said. "The rest of you can take the luggage and boxes of JESUS Film equipment outside. The missionary is supposed to meet us there with a bus. We'll join you out there."

Emily and her mother left with the rest of the group. Ethan and his dad started toward the airline office to report their missing box.

"We might have to leave without the soccer balls," Dad said.

"Oh, no! We can't go without them. Let's go back and look one more time."

"OK. But we'll have to hurry."

As Ethan and his dad headed back toward the baggage claim area, a man came running up to them. He was carrying a box with a red ribbon tied around it.

"I heard you talking about a missing box. Is this it?"

"YES!" Ethan gave his dad a high five and turned to the man. "Where did you find it?"

"It was in a pile of lost luggage."

"Thank you!" Ethan said, as he took the box. "And thank You, Jesus," he prayed.

3
Stuck in the Mud

Ethan and his father hurried outside to meet the missionary. He was helping their group load everything into a small bus.

"Yea!" cheered the group when they saw the box in Ethan's arms.

"Hello," said the missionary. "I'm Dave. Welcome to Costa Rica." He took the box from Ethan and said, "I want you to meet Roberto [roh-BAIR-toh]. He is the pastor's son. He's going to stay with us tonight. Tomorrow you will meet his parents. And tomorrow night we will show the JESUS Film in their village."

"*Hola* [OH-lah] (Hello)," Roberto said, as he took the box from Missionary Dave. He piled it on top of the duffle bags in the backseat of the bus.

"Roberto takes English classes at school," continued the missionary. "He will be your translator. He will help us understand each other's language. It will be good practice for Roberto."

When everyone was seated in the bus, the missionary started the motor. "Are you ready to go to my house and eat?"

"Yes!" everyone shouted.

The missionary served a delicious meal of chicken with rice, fresh pineapple, and mangoes. After eating, the group enjoyed visiting before going to bed. Ethan was so excited, he could hardly sleep. But before he knew it, he woke up to birds singing outside the window.

After breakfast, the group got on the bus again. Missionary Dave drove up a steep road with beautiful flowers and trees all around. As they rode along, it started to rain. Then it poured. It rained so hard that the road began to look like chocolate pudding. The missionary drove the bus from one side of the road to the other, trying to avoid the deep potholes. But suddenly, the bus slid off the road. They were stuck in the mud!

"Everybody out," Missionary Dave instructed. "We'll have to push the bus out of the mud."

Ethan and the others pushed and rocked the bus until it finally moved. Ethan looked at

his pants. He was covered with mud from his waist down. Water was running down his face. He looked around. Dad, Mom, Emily, and all the others were just as muddy.

Roberto laughed. "Now you look like us. We get stuck in the mud just about every time it rains. And it rains every day this time of year."

When the group finally arrived in Roberto's village, his parents greeted them at the door of their home. Everyone helped unload the bus, and then they got cleaned up and dried off.

Ethan opened the box of soccer balls and took out the five balls. Then he took out the air pump and showed Roberto how to use it.

"These soccer balls are really cool!" Roberto said, as he pumped air into one of them. "In my village, we make our own soccer balls by wrapping tape around wadded up plastic bags." Roberto finished pumping air into the ball, then held it up. "This doesn't look like a regular soccer ball. What do the colors mean?"

"The colors tell the story of God's Son, Jesus," explained Ethan. "Each color tells part of the story."

"Amazing!"

"What's amazing?" Ethan's dad asked, as he joined the boys.

"These soccer balls are amazing," said Roberto.

"Yes, they are," agreed Dad. "And it looks like you will soon have them ready."

4
The Game

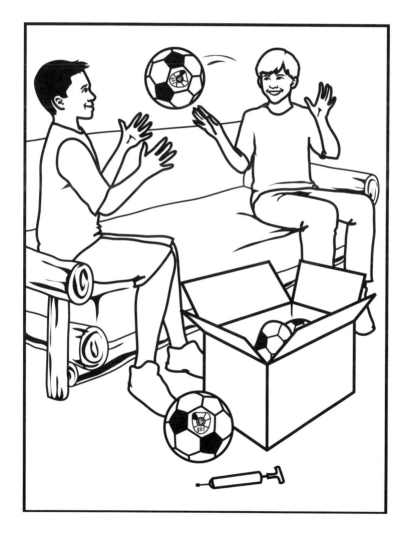

"Dad, can we play soccer now?" Ethan could hardly wait to start using the new soccer balls.

"Sure! You, Roberto, and Emily can go over to the school soccer field and play there. That's where we're going to set up the JESUS Film equipment. Be careful, though. The field still could be muddy."

"We'll be careful," Ethan said. He pumped air into the last soccer ball and tossed it to Roberto. "Let's go!"

When the three of them reached the field, Ethan said, "Well, Dad was right."

"Yeah. It does look slick, but I'm used to it," said Roberto. Just then, he saw his friends coming. "It looks like we'll have enough players for two teams." He kicked the soccer ball to one of the boys.

The boy picked up the ball and spun it around. He gave Roberto a puzzled look. "Qué es eso [KAY ehs EH-soh]?"

Roberto looked at Ethan. "He wants to know about the colors. You tell him. I'll translate what you say into Spanish."

The kids quickly gathered around Ethan. They listened carefully to Ethan as he explained the colors on the ball, and then to Roberto as he repeated it in Spanish.

When Roberto finished translating, Ethan yelled, "Are you ready to play soccer?"

"Yes!" the kids shouted, as they ran out on the field.

After kicking the ball around for a few minutes, Roberto divided the group into two teams. He appointed Emily to one team and Ethan to the other. Next, he chose goalies for each team. Then he picked a few blades of grass and hid them in his hand.

"Juanita and Mario, think of a number between 1 and 10," said Roberto. "The one who guesses how many blades of grass I have in my hand, or gets the closest, can choose to kick off first."

"Ocho [OH-choh] (eight)!" called Juanita.

"Cinco [SEEN-koh] (five)!" shouted Mario.

"Five! You guessed the exact number, Mario." Roberto showed them the five blades of grass in his hand. "Mario's team will choose."

"We choose to kick off," said Mario.

The teams quickly lined up. Ethan could tell they had played a lot of soccer by the way the

forwards and halfbacks lined up. Mario kicked the ball. Ethan ran at top speed toward the right side of the field. He kicked the ball toward the goal. But Emily blocked it and kicked the ball to Roberto. As Ethan ran toward Roberto, he slipped on the wet grass, twisting his ankle as he fell.

"Ouch!" Ethan cried in pain. "Get Dad, Emily. I think I broke my ankle."

5
The Goal

Emily ran down the street to the pastor's house. The men had just finished loading the JESUS Film equipment onto the back of an old truck. They were ready to take it to the soccer field.

"Dad! Dad! Come quick!" yelled Emily. "Ethan's hurt."

Her father and the pastor jumped into the truck and drove to the field. Emily went to find her mother.

All the kids were gathered around Ethan on the soccer field. Ethan's dad hurried over to his son and knelt beside him. "What happened?"

"I slid on the wet grass and twisted my ankle as I went down." Ethan grabbed his ankle and groaned. "It hurts, Dad."

"I'm sure it does," his dad said calmly. "Let me check it more closely." He gently moved Ethan's leg. "I don't think you broke your ankle. I think you've sprained it. A sprain can be as painful as a break. You'll have to stay off that foot for a while."

"Oh, no, Dad. I've got to finish the game."

Dad shook his head. "Maybe tomorrow you can sit on the sidelines and keep score. But now you need to rest."

Ethan's dad picked up his son and carried him to the truck. All the kids followed them. Just then, Emily and her mother arrived. Dad assured them that Ethan was OK.

"Dad, tell the kids about the JESUS Film we're going to show tonight. Roberto will translate for you."

"Good idea, Ethan." He motioned for Roberto to join him. "Boys and girls, you are invited to come and see a special film tonight about God's Son, Jesus. We're going to show it right here on the soccer field as soon as it gets dark."

"Ask your family and friends to come too," added the pastor.

"Tomorrow you can use the soccer ball to play another game," said Dad. "And afterward, Ethan will tell you what the colors mean."

"He's already told us," Mario said. "Gold is for God, who lives in heaven; black is for sin; red is for Jesus' blood; white stands for a clean heart; and I forget what green means."

After Roberto translated what Mario said, he added, "Green is for growing as a Christian."

"I'm really glad you're here to help," Ethan said to Roberto. "By the way, what is the Spanish word for goal?"

"The Spanish word sounds the same as the English word, but it's spelled g-o-l," explained Roberto.

Even though his ankle hurt, Ethan felt good inside. He was glad he came to Costa Rica to tell others about Jesus. Telling people about Jesus was more fun than making a *gol* in a soccer game.

Fun Things To Do

1. Find Costa Rica on a map.

2. Draw a soccer ball. Color it with colors that tell the story of Jesus.
   Gold: God/heaven
   Black: Sin
   Red: Jesus' blood
   White: Clean heart
   Green: Growing in love for God and others

3. Tell someone what the colors on the ball mean.

4. Talk to your missions leader about ordering the special soccer ball from www.JFHP.org.

5. Find out if anyone in your church is planning to go on a mission trip. Then talk to your parents about your family going on the trip.

6. Talk to your missions leader about sending a letter or email to your church's LINKS missionary.

7. Pray for your LINKS missionary.

8. See how many of the Spanish words in this story you can remember.